W9-AYF-355

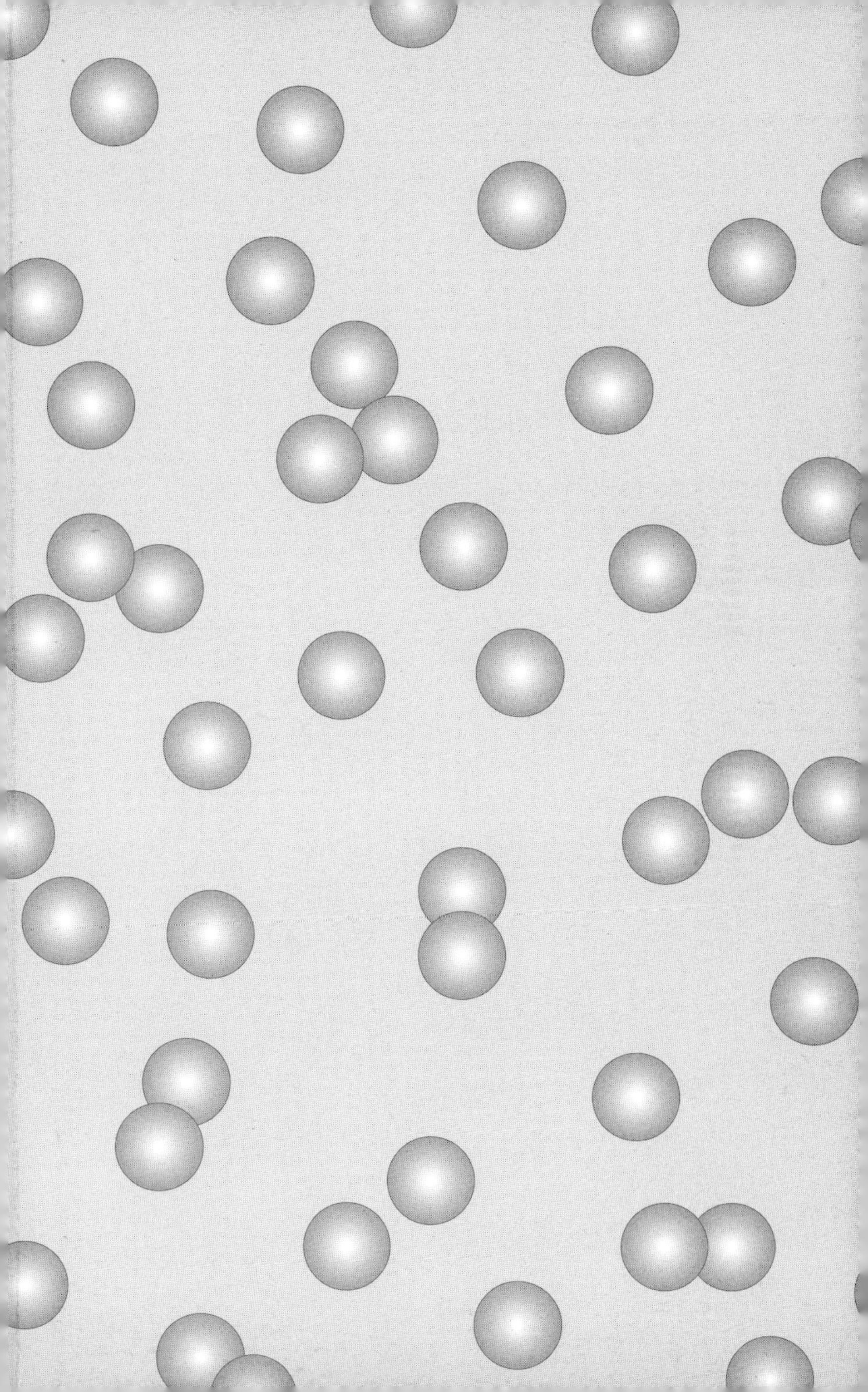

Tommy Trouble and the Magic Marble

Tommy Trouble and the Magic Marble

by

RALPH FLETCHER

Illustrated by

BEN CALDWELL

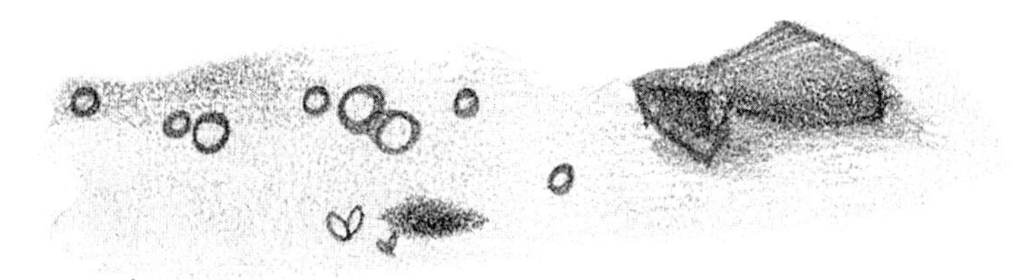

Henry Holt and Company • New York

Henry Holt and Company, LLC
Publishers since 1866
115 West 18th Street, New York, New York 10011

Henry Holt is a registered trademark of Henry Holt and Company, LLC

Published in Canada by Fitzhenry & Whiteside Ltd.,
195 Allstate Parkway, Markham, Ontario L3R 4T8.
Library of Congress Cataloging-in-Publication Data
Fletcher, Ralph J.
Tommy Trouble and the magic marble / by Ralph Fletcher;
illustrated by Ben Caldwell.
p. cm.
Summary: Five-year-old Bradley tries to help big brother Tommy
earn enough money to buy a magnificent marble for his collection.
[1. Brothers—Fiction. 2. Moneymaking projects—Fiction.
3. Marbles (Game objects)—Fiction. 4. Collectors and collecting—Fiction.]
I. Caldwell, Ben, ill. II. Title.
PZ7.F634To 2000 [Fic]—dc21 99-40727
ISBN 0-8050-6387-0 / First Edition—2000
Printed in the United States of America on acid-free paper. ∞
1 3 5 7 9 10 8 6 4 2

For Robert and Joseph,
who heard this story first

—R. F.

For Thomas, Evan, Patrick, and Kelvin

—B. C.

Contents

1. The Crystal Mumbo Jumbo
1

2. Flowers for Sale
9

3. The Time-out Rug
16

4. The Snake
22

5. Playing with Fire
30

6. The Alien
40

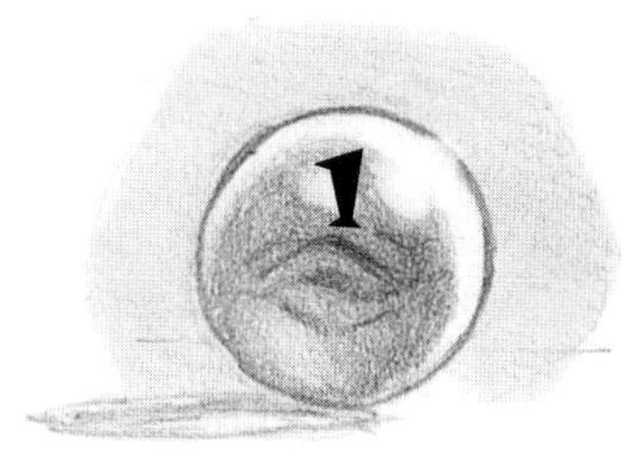

The Crystal Mumbo Jumbo

Tommy loved to collect stuff. He kept his collections in special boxes under his bed. Tommy collected rocks, crystals, and fossils. He collected baseball cards. He collected coins and paper money from around the world.

He collected some pretty peculiar things, too. He had a collection of hubcaps, fourteen of them, he found on the side of the road. He had another collection of used-up Band-Aid bandages, most of them stained with blood. Mom wanted him to throw them away, but Tommy thought they were cool.

But Tommy's marbles were his favorites. He

loved the different sizes and colors, the way they sparkled in the light. He loved the little click-click-clicks they made when he poured them out of the cloth bag where he kept them. He knew exactly how many he had: eight peewees, twenty-two cat's-eyes, eleven bogies, and three crystal bogies.

But today he counted only seven peewees. He counted again. One marble was missing.

"BRADLEY!" Tommy screamed.

A moment later his little brother ran into his room. "What?" Bradley asked.

"Give me back my marble," Tommy said.

"NO WAY!" Bradley yelled as he darted out of the room. Tommy jumped up and started racing after him. Bradley was only five years old, but he was fast. Tommy chased him through the kitchen, out the back door, and around the house. He didn't catch him until they got to the front yard.

"Give it back!" Tommy reached into Bradley's front pocket and pulled out the pee-wee.

"It's not fair!" Bradley squealed. "You've got a million marbles! I only took one!"

"You should have asked," Tommy said.

"You would have said no," Bradley told him.

"True," Tommy admitted. "But you should have asked anyway."

"Look! There's Spencer," said Bradley.

Spencer Ross was coming down the street. He was throwing something into the air and catching it as he walked. Tommy didn't like

Spencer Ross. Spencer was big and tough. And he could be mean.

"Hiya, guys," Spencer said. He threw a small ball into the air and caught it.

"Hi," Tommy said. "What's that?"

Spencer handed the ball to Tommy. "Don't drop it," Spencer said. It was the biggest glass marble Tommy had ever seen.

"Take a really good look at it," Spencer told

him. “That’s one of the rarest marbles in the world. Take a good look at it. Go ahead. Put it up to your eye.”

Tommy looked deep inside the marble. The glass was blue and clear. He could see a tiny silver net at the very center.

“That marble is magic,” Spencer said.

“What kind of magic?” Tommy asked.

“The net is the magic part,” Spencer explained.

"Let's say you have bad dreams or nightmares, right? Well, that magic net catches them so they don't bother you anymore."

"You want to trade?" Tommy asked. "I'll give you three crystal bogies for it."

"Crystal bogies!" Spencer laughed and grabbed the marble out of Tommy's hand. "Ha!

Who needs crystal bogies? I've got millions of them! *This* is a crystal mumbo jumbo! You won't find another one like it in the whole world. I won't trade, but I might sell it."

"How much?"

"Ten bucks," Spencer said.

"Ten bucks!" Tommy whistled.

"Take it or leave it," Spencer said. "Do you have the money?"

"Not now," Tommy said. "But I know I can get it."

"You get the money, and I'll sell it to you," Spencer told him. "But you'd better hurry. I know another kid who wants to buy it if you don't."

"I'll get the money," Tommy said.

"You sure?" Spencer asked.

"Definitely," Tommy told him.

"Here," Spencer said. He tossed the crystal mumbo jumbo to Tommy.

Tommy was so surprised he almost dropped it. "Why are you giving it to me?" he asked.

"I'm not giving it to you," Spencer said. "I'm letting you hold it. I'll come back after lunch. If you get the money, you can keep it. If not, you give it back to me."

"Cool," Tommy said.

"Take real good care of it," Spencer told Tommy. "That's a crystal mumbo jumbo. I'm warning you—if anything happens to my marble, you're dead meat."

"Don't worry," Tommy said as he watched Spencer walk away.

Flowers for Sale

Tommy stared at the crystal mumbo jumbo. It glowed like a huge diamond in his hand. He couldn't believe Spencer had left it with him.

"How much is ten bucks?" Bradley asked.

"Ten dollars," Tommy told him. "I've got two dollars, so I need eight more. Do you have any money?"

"Yeah!" Bradley said. "I got lots!"

"How much?" Tommy asked.

"I got five pennies!" Bradley said proudly.

"Five pennies! I need eight hundred pennies!"

"Oh," Bradley said. "Hey, can I hold it? Please?"

"What if you drop it, and it breaks?" Tommy asked. "Spencer will pulverize me."

"But I'll be so, so careful!" Bradley said.

Just then Mrs. Snickenberger, who lived down the street, waved as she drove past. As Tommy waved at Mrs. Snickenberger, he got an idea.

"Okay, here's what I'll do," Tommy said to Bradley. "I'll let you hold the marble if you do something real easy. All you have to do is help me pick some of Mom's flowers. Follow me!"

They ran straight to Mom's garden and started to pick.

"This *is* easy!" Bradley said.

"Pick lots," Tommy said. "Forget about the yellow ones. Just pick the red ones."

"Ow!" Bradley cried. "They've got prickers!"

"Keep picking," Tommy told him.

"Here." Bradley handed the flowers to Tommy. "Can I hold the marble now?"

"Not yet," Tommy said. They put all the flowers together into a big bunch and started walking down the street.

"Where are we going?" Bradley asked.

"Mrs. Snickenberger's house," Tommy said. When they reached the house, Tommy handed the crystal mumbo jumbo to Bradley and rang the doorbell. Mrs. Snickenberger came to the door.

"Hi, Mrs. Snickenberger," Tommy said.

"Roses!" Mrs. Snickenberger exclaimed. "Oh, I simply adore roses!"

"We're selling them for eight dollars," Tommy told her.

"That seems like a fair price for such pretty flowers," she said. "Wait here while I get the money." She went inside.

"Look!" Bradley said. It was Mom. She was coming down the street and she was walking fast.

"Hey, Mom!" Bradley yelled. "We're selling flowers!"

"You're selling *my* flowers." Mom shook her head. "My prize roses! How could you, Tommy?"

"I need the money to buy a marble from Spencer," Tommy said.

"It's a crystal mumbo jumbo," Bradley explained. He held it up and showed it to her. "It's magic!"

"You should have asked my permission," Mom said.

"You would have said no," Tommy said.

"True," she admitted. "But you should have asked anyway. My flowers are *not* for sale."

Mrs. Snickenberger came back outside and smiled at Mom. "Look at these beautiful roses your boys brought me," she said. She gave Tommy eight dollars. "Here you go, Tommy."

Mom took the money from Tommy and gave it back to Mrs. Snickenberger. "I'm sorry," Mom said. "Tommy had no business selling you my flowers. Isn't that right, Tommy?"

"It's not all my fault," Tommy said. He pointed at Bradley. "He picked them, too!"

"You told me to!" Bradley cried.

"I think I need to have a talk with these boys," Mom said.

Mrs. Snickenberger looked a bit confused.

"Well, I guess I should give these flowers back to you."

"No, I want you to have them," Mom said. "Please."

"Really?" Mrs. Snickenberger was delighted. "Well, thank you! They sure are pretty."

"We'd better go home now," Mom said.

"Don't be too hard on them," Mrs. Snickenberger said. "You know what they say. Boys will be boys."

The Time-out Rug

In the living room Tommy sat on the time-out rug. Mom made him sit there whenever he got into trouble. He hated it. The rug was small and old and it smelled like trouble.

Tommy sat there listening to sounds outside the window. He heard an airplane fly over the house. Then a car drove past. He heard Bradley playing in the backyard. They had a stream and lots of woods behind their house. It was a great place for playing hide-and-seek or capture-the-flag. Now he could hear Bradley and some other kids singing a silly song. They sang it over and over.

"Buzz bug, critter critter,
Buzz bug, critter critter."

Tommy didn't want to be stuck inside sitting on a smelly rug. He wanted to go play outside.

Mom came out of the kitchen. "Do you have something to say?" she asked.

"I'm sorry," Tommy said. "But it's not fair, Mom. How come I got in trouble but Bradley didn't? He picked flowers, too."

"Bradley is five years old," Mom said. "You're almost nine. You're old enough to know better. Right?"

"I guess," he answered. "I said I'm sorry. Can I go now?"

"Not yet," she said. "I want you to think about what you did wrong."

Tommy tried to think about it. But all he could think about was the crystal mumbo jumbo. It was sitting on the desk in his bedroom. He wished he could hold it right now. He thought about how nice and heavy and smooth it would feel in his hands. He remembered the way it shined, like it was lit from the inside, when he held it up to the light.

"A crystal mumbo jumbo," Tommy whispered to himself. "A magic crystal mumbo jumbo."

He wanted it so badly, but how on earth would he ever get eight dollars?

He wondered if it really was magic. Spencer said it was, but Spencer didn't always tell the truth. One time Tommy brought a sandwich to the park. Spencer was there. He asked if he could have a bite. He promised he would only take a little bite but, when Tommy gave him the sandwich, Spencer stuffed the whole thing into his mouth.

Tommy looked out the window. Sunlight was coming through the glass, and he could see tiny bits of dust playing in the light.

"I'll have to sit here for a million years," he said out loud, even though nobody could hear him.

To make the time pass, Tommy started playing a game. He closed his eyes and pretended that the time-out rug was a leaf. He was a caterpillar curled up in the middle of it.

Then he pretended that the rug was a lily pad floating in a pond. He was a big bullfrog sitting on his pad. He caught bugs for lunch with his long, sticky tongue.

Pretty soon he got tired of eating bugs, so he turned the time-out rug into a magic carpet. He lay down and held tight to the edge as it sped through the air. Whoosh! The carpet was fast! He flew so high that when he looked down his house looked like a little toy. He swooped down over Spencer Ross's house. If Spencer could only

see him now! But suddenly he realized he was heading straight toward a dark storm cloud. He saw a huge fork of lightning.

"OH NO!" he cried. He leaned to one side and the carpet swerved, just missing the storm cloud. Then he pointed the magic carpet up and zoomed into outer space.

Mom came into the living room. "Have you thought about what you did wrong?" she asked.

He nodded.

"All right," she said. "You can go now. Please stay out of trouble."

"I will," Tommy said, and ran outside.

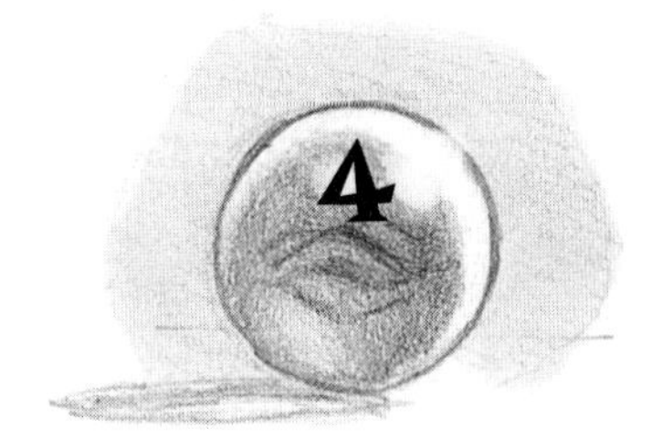

The Snake

As soon as Tommy came outside, Bradley ran over to him.

"Let me hold that oogie boogie," Bradley said.

"What are you talking about?" Tommy asked.

"You know, the oogie boogie," Bradley said. "Spencer's marble."

"It's not an oogie boogie. It's a mumbo jumbo," Tommy told him. "No! And you can't hold it. Don't bug me!"

Tommy sat down on the grass to think. Where was he going to get the eight dollars? He thought about selling one of his other collections. He wondered if he could sell his hubcaps.

But who would pay eight dollars for a bunch of old and dented hubcaps?

"Tommy, look!" Bradley cried. "A snake! A real snake!"

"Don't move!" Tommy yelled. He ran over to the edge of the stream to look where Bradley was pointing. It was a snake, all right, sitting on a flat rock. The snake was green, with a black

stripe running down its side. It looked up and stuck out a skinny tongue.

"Cool!" Tommy said. "He's a garter snake. Dad told me all about them, so I know what they look like. They're not poisonous or anything."

"You sure?" Bradley asked.

"Positive. Wait, I've got an idea." Tommy ran back to the garage, found a box, and carried the box back to the little stream.

"What are you going to do?" Bradley asked.

"Watch," Tommy said. He climbed down to the water and put the box under the snake. "Yah! Shoo! Yow! Scat!"

He waved his arm near the snake, and it fell right smack into the box. Tommy closed the top so the snake couldn't get out.

"Got him!" Bradley cried. "We got him!"

"Yup!" Tommy said.

"He's mine," Bradley said. "I found him."

"I got him into the box," Tommy said.

"I saw him first!" Bradley said. "He's mine!"

"Oh, all right," Tommy said.

"Hey, look at your shoes," Bradley said.

Tommy looked down. Both of his shoes were soaking wet.

"Mom will be mad," Bradley said.

"The sun will dry them out," Tommy said. He started to untie his shoe, but right then he spotted Spencer Ross walking toward them.

"Hiya," he said, brushing the top of his head. His hair had been cut short and flat on the top. "Pretty cool haircut, huh? You guys should get a buzz cut like this."

Tommy and Bradley didn't say anything.

"They give you this kind of haircut when you join the marines," Spencer explained. "My dad was in the marines. My grandpa was, too. And I'm going to join when I'm old enough. You've got to be real tough to be in the marines."

"You said you were coming back this afternoon," Tommy said.

"Changed my mind," Spencer said. "Still got my crystal mumbo jumbo?"

"Yeah," Tommy said.

"Good." Spencer pointed at the box. "Hey, what do you have in there?"

“A snake,” Bradley said. “We just caught him.” Tommy opened the box. Spencer leaned down to get a good look. Then he reached in and picked up the snake. The snake curled his body around Spencer’s arm. It looked like he had a green rope wrapped around him.

“I think he likes me,” Spencer said. “Hey, I got an idea. I’ll trade you my crystal mumbo jumbo for this snake.”

Tommy couldn’t believe his ears.

"What do you say?" Spencer asked. "It's the perfect trade. I get the snake, you get the crystal mumbo jumbo."

"It's a deal!" Tommy said with a big smile. But Bradley was shaking his head.

"No," Bradley said.

"Why not?" Tommy asked.

"Because," Bradley told him. "I'm not trading it for anything."

Spencer looked at Tommy.

"Are you going to let that little squirt push you around?"

"C'mon, Bradley!" Tommy said. "We're going to trade!"

"He's *my* snake," Bradley said. "I found him."

"It's a *great* deal," Spencer said. "You won't find another crystal mumbo jumbo anywhere in the world."

"Come on, Bradley!" Tommy begged. "I'll let you hold the marble whenever you want."

"Nope." Bradley shook his head.

"It can be half yours, half mine," Tommy told his brother.

"No!" Bradley took the snake from Spencer and put him back into the box.

"Suit yourself," Spencer told Tommy. "I'll be back tomorrow morning, early. You give me this snake, or twelve bucks, if you want the marble."

"Twelve bucks!" Tommy cried. "But you said ten!"

"The price just went up," Spencer said with a mean laugh. "I hope you take good care of it. If anything happens to it, you're dead meat. *Double* dead meat."

"Don't worry," Tommy said.

"What's wrong with you?" Tommy asked his brother when Spencer left. "Are you crazy? It's the perfect trade!"

"I don't want him to have my snake," Bradley said. He turned the box over and dumped out the snake.

"Don't!" Tommy yelled. But before he could stop it, the snake had slithered through the grass and disappeared.

"You are so stupid!" Tommy told his brother. "I can't believe you did that!"

Playing with Fire

Tommy stomped into the house, went straight to his bedroom, and slammed the door. He took out the crystal mumbo jumbo and held it up to the window. He put it up to his eye and stared at the little silver net in the middle.

He didn't want to give it back to Spencer. He wanted to keep it for himself, forever. But now that Bradley had let the snake go, he needed ten dollars to buy the marble. Ten dollars!

Tommy thought and thought. Finally he got an idea. As soon as Bradley came into the house, Tommy tiptoed outside. He went back to the stream to look for the snake.

He looked everywhere. He searched under logs. He checked the deep grass. He climbed down to the place where Bradley first saw the snake. Nothing. All Tommy found was a pile of smooth stones. He needed ten dollars, so now he counted out ten stones.

"One dollar." He threw a rock over the stream and into the woods.

"Two dollars," he said, and threw another rock.

That's when he heard the sound. A buzzing sound. Bees! He could see bees flying in and out of a hole in a dead tree.

"What are you doing?"

Tommy turned around and saw his brother.

"Don't follow me," he said. "Go back home."

"You can't make me," Bradley said. "Hey, that's a beehive, Tommy. I bet they're making honey."

"Duh!" Tommy said. "Of course it's a beehive! Watch this." Tommy threw one stone at the beehive. It just missed.

"Don't do that, Tommy!"

"You're not afraid of a couple of wimpy little bees, are you?" Tommy asked.

He threw a second stone at the tree. That one missed, too. Tommy threw another rock. This one hit the tree—THWOCK!—right under the beehive.

"Stop it, Tommy!" Bradley yelled.

Bees started pouring out of the hole. Soon there was a swarm of them all around the tree. One bee buzzed close to Bradley. Then another. Then another.

"Don't move," Tommy whispered.

"OWWWW!" Bradley screamed. "OWW! I got stung! I got stung!" He started running toward home.

"Bradley!" Tommy cried. He dropped the stones and ran after his brother.

"OWWW! OWWW! OWWW!" Bradley screamed. He ran up the back steps into the kitchen, with Tommy right behind.

"I got stung! I got stung!" Bradley yelled. He was holding his eye and jumping up and down.

Mom knelt down and looked at Bradley's face. "He got stung right below his eye!" Mom said.

"How did that happen?" asked Dad.

"Tommy threw a rock at the beehive!" Bradley cried.

"You did what?" Dad and Mom stared at Tommy.

"You know that bees are dangerous, don't you?" Dad asked.

"Yes," Tommy said in a small voice.

"How many times have I told you that?" Dad said. "Never, ever play near a beehive. You play with bees and you're playing with fire."

Tommy looked at his brother. The side of Bradley's face was so puffed up, it was hard to see his eye.

When Tommy saw Bradley's eye, he started to cry. That made Bradley start crying again.

"Let's get in the car," Dad said. "I want the doctor to look at that eye."

"Tommy, do you want to come to the doctor's or stay home?" Mom asked him.

"Stay home," Tommy mumbled.

Mrs. Snickenberger came to stay with Tommy while Mom and Dad took Bradley to the doctor. Tommy stood at the window in the living room and watched as the car drove away.

Mrs. Snickenberger sat on the couch. "Would you like to sit over here?" she asked Tommy. "We could play a game of cards if you like."

"No thanks," Tommy said. He sat down on the time-out rug. In the middle of that rug he felt like he was sitting in the bull's-eye of a target. A target for trouble.

"Can I get you something to eat?" Mrs. Snickenberger asked.

"No thanks."

"I guess you're worried about your brother," she said.

Tommy nodded. He closed his eyes and pictured Spencer walking down the street, throwing the crystal mumbo jumbo into the air. He wished he had never seen either one of them.

When he heard the car in the driveway, Tommy jumped off the rug and ran to the door.

"Is Bradley going to be all right?" he asked.

"Yes," Mom said. "The doctor put medicine on his eye to help the swelling go down."

"Right now he needs to sleep," said Dad.

Bradley went to bed.

Mom made supper, but Tommy couldn't eat.

"You haven't touched your food," Mom said. She pointed at his plate.

"I can't eat, Mom," he said. "I hate how his eye looks."

"I know," Mom said. "The doctor promised it would be better tomorrow morning."

That night Tommy had a dream. Bradley was sitting on a couch watching TV. At first his face looked like it always did. Then one of Bradley's eyes began to swell. The other one puffed up, too. His nose got fat, his ears got big, and his whole head puffed up like a balloon. Bradley's head got bigger and bigger until it looked like it was about to explode.

"NO!" Tommy yelled.

He sat up in bed. He reached over and turned on the light. Bradley was sleeping. One eye was still puffy, but the rest of his face looked okay.

"Just a bad dream," Tommy said to himself. He pulled the covers up around Bradley. Then he got back into bed, turned off the light, and fell asleep.

The Alien

When Tommy woke the next morning, he saw Bradley standing in front of the mirror, looking at himself.

"Don't you think I look kind of weird?" Bradley asked.

"Yeah," Tommy admitted. "But your eye looks a lot better. Does it still hurt?"

"Nope," Bradley said. "Hey, where's that crystal mumbo jumbo? Can I hold it?"

Tommy took the big marble off his desk and handed it to Bradley.

"It's not magic," Tommy said.

"How do you know?" Bradley asked.

"Spencer said that little net is supposed to capture all your bad dreams, right? Well, it doesn't work. I had a nightmare last night that really freaked me out."

Bradley held the marble up to his good eye.

"Well, maybe it's not magic, but it's still awesome," Bradley said.

Just then the doorbell rang.

"That must be Spencer," Tommy said. "C'mon, let's go talk to him. You can carry the marble." Tommy ran out of the bedroom and opened the front door. Bradley ran after him.

"What happened to you?" Spencer said when he saw Bradley. "You look like an alien."

"A bee stung me," Bradley said.

"You can say that again," Spencer said.

"A bee stung me," Bradley said.

“He kind of talks like an alien, too.” Spencer looked at Tommy. “Come outside.”

Tommy followed Spencer out onto the side-walk. Bradley followed Tommy.

“I didn’t say for the alien to come,” Spencer said.

“I’m not an alien!” Bradley cried.

“Yeah, he’s my brother,” Tommy told Spencer.

"Whatever. Well, you got something for me?"

"Nope. The snake got away."

"Tough luck," Spencer said. "You got the money?"

"Nope, I've only got two bucks," Tommy said. "Besides, I don't think your marble has any magic."

"What are you talking about?" Spencer said.

"You said it keeps away bad dreams, but last night I had a real nightmare. Here." Tommy took the marble from Bradley and gave it to Spencer. "Maybe it needs a new battery."

Bradley laughed.

"You think that's funny?" Spencer asked Bradley.

"Yeah," Bradley said. He smiled at Tommy.

"You guys are losers," Spencer said. He threw the marble into the air and caught it.

"That's what you think," Tommy said as Spencer walked away.

"Too bad," Bradley said.

"Forget about him," Tommy said. "Let's play marbles."

"Okay, cool!" Bradley said.

Tommy ran into the house, pulled his bag of marbles out from under his bed, and hurried back outside. He took a marble out of the bag. "Hey, Bradley," he said. "This one is magic."

"Like Spencer's marble?" Bradley asked.

"No!" Tommy replied, making a funny face. "This one isn't fake magic like Spencer's marble. This one is mega-magic! It will turn all the other marbles into firecrackers and cherry bombs! So they start, like, blowing up all over the place!"

They both laughed.

"C'mon, let's play" said Tommy.

"I go first!" Bradley said.

"Sorry," Tommy said, shaking his head. "Aliens go last. Humans go first. I'm a human, so I go first."

"TOMMY! I'M NOT AN ALIEN!"

"Okay, just kidding," Tommy said. "Go ahead and shoot."

Bradley threw his marble. It rolled over the grass, into the dirt circle, and fell right into the hole.

"Great shot," Tommy said.

"A hole in one!" Bradley yelled. "Let's see you beat that!"

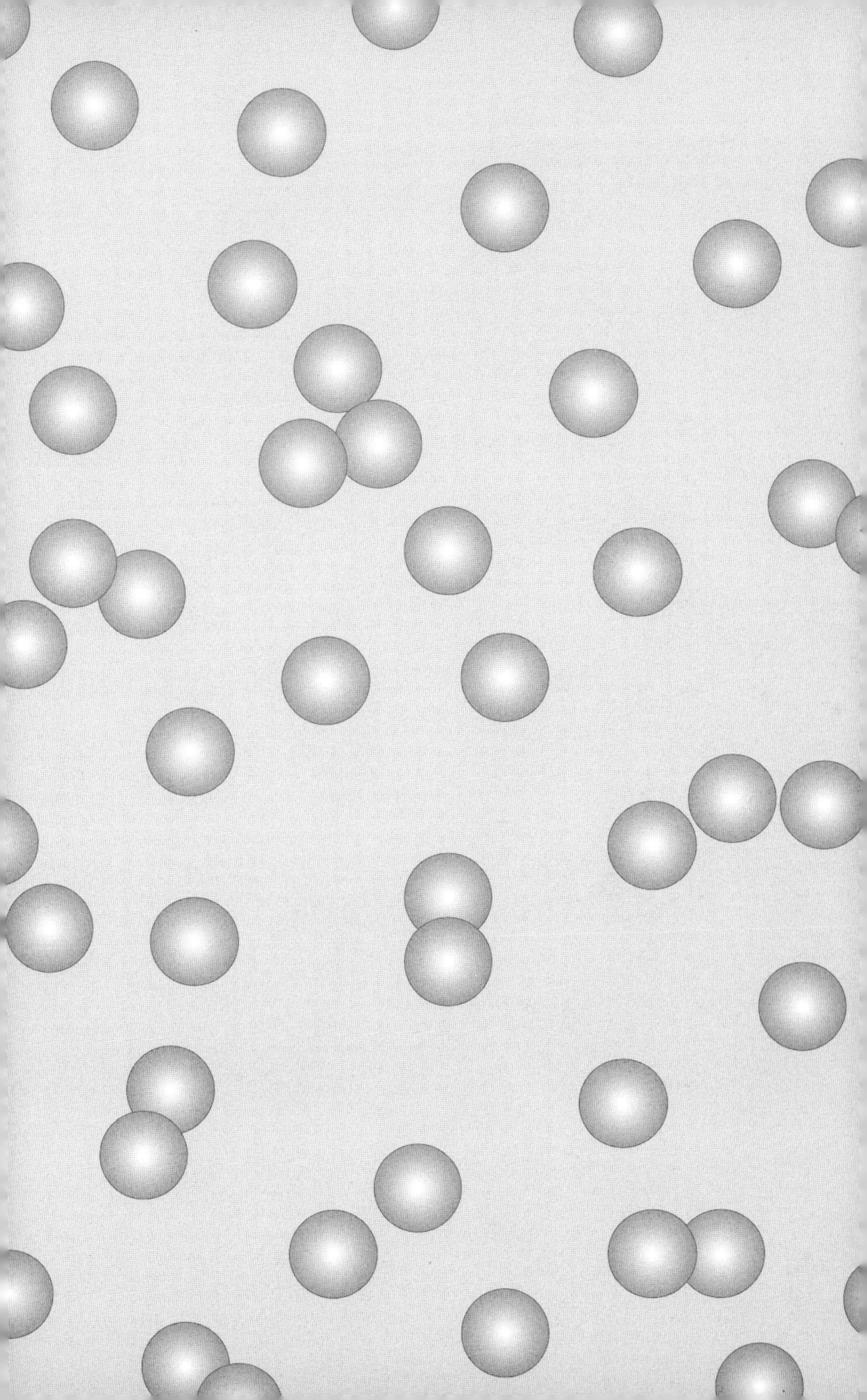